A Halloween Story

INTRODUCTION

Three friends set out on Halloween night, looking to fill their pumpkins and bags with treats of all kinds. The girls expect to have a lot of fun, but someone else is planning their own fun, and it's not to the benefit of the trick-or-treaters.

ACKNOWLEDGEMENTS

Pixabay, Creazella, and Public Domain Images for generously providing me with images needed to create the storyboard for this book.

Thanks to Jefferson of First Editing for editing this book. Your services are greatly appreciated.

FROM THE AUTHOR

I really enjoyed putting this little book together for Halloween. I hope you enjoy the story as much as I did writing it. And to all of the children going out on that fun night, "Have a safe and happy Halloween."

It was a nice evening in Littleville as three children set out for a night of fun. Lily, Abby, and Dolly were three good friends. They did everything together. Tonight they were going trick-or-treating. They had just left their first house for the night, and the old lady who lived there had given them treats. The old lady lived alone and never had children of her own. She loved kids, and on Halloween, they came from all over town to her door.

All of the usual Halloween regulars were out tonight, too. There were ghosts, witches, skeletons, vampires, mummies, and many scary monsters that hadn't shown up yet. Not all of them were bad. Some of them liked to frighten the children, while others were good and liked to watch them as they went from house to house.

Two mean ghosts were out prowling that night, Screamer and Chaser. Chaser always appeared on the scene first. He took a look around to see how many kids would be out that night. The more kids there were, the more fun he and Screamer had.

Screamer was the other mean ghost. He was so mean he even scared the monsters and other ghosts. The scarecrows were the ones he really liked to scare because they couldn't move very fast. Tonight he was picking on Mr. Stitches. Mr. Stitches moved very slowly, and it took him a while to get over the fence and get away from Screamer. When he finally got over the fence, he hid in the grass so Screamer couldn't find him.

Smiley was a friendly ghost. He never bothered the kids or tried to scare them. He loved helping them on Halloween night. He would watch them walking by with their treats and would stay close to them so Screamer and Chaser wouldn't come and steal the treats.

Though Smiley was no match for Screamer and Chaser, he would trick them by making them mad so they would chase him. This allowed the kids to escape while the ghosts were distracted.

Mr. Skeleton had slept all year long. This Halloween night, he came out of his grave to have some fun. He wanted to scare the children as they walked by. With only the moonlight shining down on him, he knew he would do a good job of scaring them tonight. "Hee, haw, haw," *he* chuckled.

Mr. Skelton jumped up on his headstone. He was so happy when he looked all around and saw that he was the only skeleton with all his parts. The rest of his long-lost dead friends only had their heads. He felt sorry for them, but he wasn't going to let that stop him from enjoying his night. He was free for one night only, and he had every intention of having fun. He jumped down from his headstone and disappeared into the night.

Witches and scarecrows were out that night as well. They didn't bother anyone, especially the scarecrows, who just stood in the fields. Jumper the scarecrow would watch the trick-or-treaters go by. He enjoyed Halloween because he got to see other scarecrows that looked like him.

Mabel, an old witch, kept busy collecting skulls to make a brew. Every Halloween, she made a big pot of witch's brew to share with her witch neighbors. The witches loved Mabel's brew because she knew how to collect skulls that would make it taste good.

Lily, Abby, and Dolly walked along the path, going from house to house. They didn't see Chaser hovering behind them. He wanted to scare them enough to make them drop their treats and run away. Chaser loved candy. He stole the children's treats because he couldn't go to the houses and get his own, and tonight he planned to get his treats the same way he did every year.

Lily, Abby, and Dolly saw their classmates Billy and Susie, who were also out trick-or-treating. The children's parents watched them from not too far away. Billy was dressed up as Frankenstein. Showing off, as usual, he pretended to scare Susie, but she was more annoyed than scared.

Susie rushed ahead of Billy. She was getting tired of his constant teasing. She was walking so fast that she didn't realize how far behind he was.

Meanwhile, Billy wasn't playing games anymore. Screamer had snuck up behind him and was chasing him. Billy tried to run, but his pants were too tight and slowed him down. He was the one scared now. He ran as fast as he could to catch up to his friend Susie.

Lily, Abby, and Dolly could hear Billy's screams just ahead of them on the road. They tried to catch up to Billy and Susie to find out what was going on.

"I wonder why Billy is screaming?" Dolly said as she stared at her friends for answers.

"He sounds like he saw a ghost," Lily said.

"Yeah," Abby chimed in. "I'll bet he did."

When Lily, Abby, and Dolly caught up with their school friends, Chaser was gone.

"Why were you screaming, Billy?" Lily asked.

When Billy told her, they all laughed because they knew they had guessed right. The friends continued chuckling as they walked to each house, looking for treats. Some homeowners would leave the treats outside for the trick-or-treaters. They would refill the pumpkin containers after the children left.

The friends came upon a house that looked so scary they didn't want to go near it. But Dolly wasn't scared of anything, and she told her friends so.

"Come on, everyone. The house is not that scary. Let's go and have a look."

The children were still afraid, but they decided to go along with Dolly anyway.

As they got closer to the house, they could see all the monsters and ghosts hovering around it. Dracula stood in the yard, staring at them. He had an angry look on his face.

"Are you sure we should go in there?" Lily asked her friends.

"Yes, it'll be fun," Dolly said. "Don't be such scaredy cats."

"I don't think we should go in there," Billy said, frightened by all the ghosts and Dracula standing outside.

"Let's not go in there," Abby said. "Let's turn around and go back."

"Ah," Dolly said. "You guys are no fun at all. Maybe we can get lots of treats at this house."

"You can go by yourself," Susie said. "I'm not going in there, either, so that's four against one that we turn around and go to another house."

"Then I'll go by myself," Dolly said. With determination, she left her friends behind and walked towards the house.

Dracula rushed over to Dolly when he saw her coming. "Get out of here, child," he said. "This is private property. You can't come in here."

"But it's Halloween," Dolly said. "Isn't your house all decorated for trick-or-treaters?" Dolly wasn't scared of Dracula because she knew he wasn't real. She knew he was the owner of the house and was dressed up as Dracula for Halloween.

Just then, Ripper, one of the ghosts hovering over the house, flew down in a mad rush behind Dracula. Dracula reached back to stop him from getting close to Dolly. "Get back, Ripper! I'll handle this."

Dracula looked sternly at Dolly. "You'd better get out of here before Ripper gets you. He is very angry, and I can't keep him back much longer."

Dolly was upset as she left the house. She still didn't believe the ghosts were real, but then she heard Abby screaming. Abby was pointing at the sky and watching the ghosts and mummy coming towards them. She warned Dolly to hurry up.

Dolly started to run when she saw the ghosts. She was so scared she tripped and fell. When she got back up, she realized she had dropped some of her treats.

She wanted to go back and get them, but there was no way she was going to make those mean ghosts madder. She realized now that she had been wrong; the ghosts and Dracula were very real.

The friends were still out of breath from running when they came upon some trick-or-treaters heading towards the haunted house, where Dracula was still standing outside.

Abby called out to the trick-or-treaters, "Don't go to that house. The monsters and ghosts are real and very mean. There's a nice house across the road. We got lots of treats there." She pointed to a house far away from the haunted house.

"We weren't going to that creepy house," one of the kids said. "It looks way too spooky for us."

Except for Dolly going to the haunted house and upsetting the ghosts, the girls had had a nice evening with Billy and Susie, who by now had left for home because they were so scared. Lily, Abby, and Dolly decided to go home, too. They had lots of treats because, during the night, they had brought their treats home and then gone back out and filled up their pumpkins again.

As they started walking home, Mr. Skeleton and the mean ghosts Screamer and Chaser showed up. They tried to frighten the girls and take their treats. But Smiley was flying by and saw what was happening. He summoned his many friends to come and scare away the mean ghosts and Mr. Skeleton. The girls liked Smiley. He had been hanging around them for most of the night.

Once the girls were home and safely tucked in their beds, the night outside grew quiet again. The ghosts and monsters, along with the witches, mummies, scarecrows, skeletons, and Dracula, were going back to their caves and hiding places for another year.

Screamer and Chaser had enjoyed scaring the children. They had stolen lots of candy out of the children's pumpkins when they weren't looking. They picked up all of the candy and left for home.

All in all, everyone had a fun night in the town of Littleville. And when the clock struck midnight, the ghosts, witches, skeletons, Dracula, and all of the monsters, good and bad, were gone. Only the scarecrows remained, standing still once more as they waited for another year to pass. Then Halloween would be back, and all the fun would begin again.

The End

A Halloween Story

By Patsy Whittle

Copyright 2020